Pack a Bag!

Suzanne I. Barchers

Consultants

Robert C. Calfee, Ph.D.
Stanford University

P. David Pearson, Ph.D.
University of California, Berkeley

Publishing Credits

Dona Herweck Rice, *Editor-in-Chief*
Lee Aucoin, *Creative Director*
Sharon Coan, M.S.Ed., *Project Manager*
Jamey Acosta, *Editor*
Robin Erickson, *Interior Layout Designer*
Cathie Lowmiller, *Illustrator*
Robin Demougeot, *Associate Art Director*
Heather Marr, *Copy Editor*
Rachelle Cracchiolo, M.S.Ed., Publisher

Teacher Created Materials

5301 Oceanus Drive
Huntington Beach, CA 92649-1030
http://www.tcmpub.com

ISBN 978-1-4333-2409-3

© 2012 by Teacher Created Materials, Inc.

BP 5028

I put gas in the van.
We can go see Jan.
Pack what you can.

I can pack a ball. I
can pack ten jacks.

I can pack a sack.
Can I add a yak?

I can pack a fan. I can pack a hat.

I can pack a cap.
Can I add a cat?

I can pack a mitt. I
can pack a bat.

I can pack a sax.
Can I add a rat?

I can pack a yam. I
can pack a ham.

I can pack some jam.
Can I add a pan?

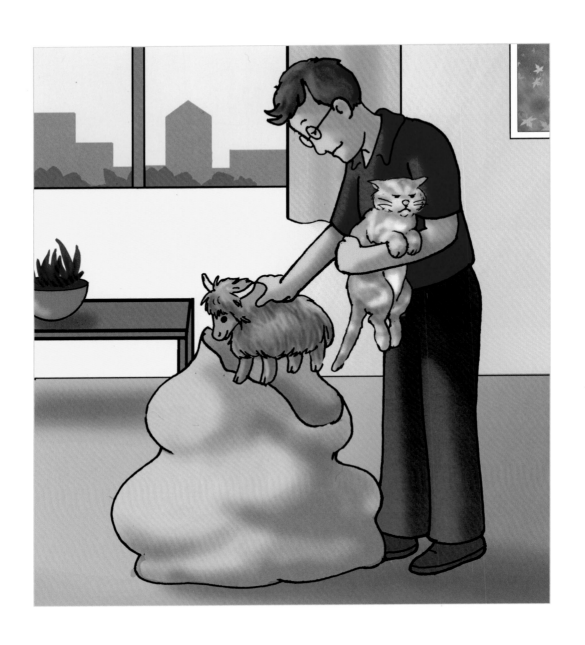

Do not pack a yak.
Do not pack a cat.

Do not pack a rat.
Do not pack a pan.

San!   I can pack San!

Decodable Words

add	hat	rat
bag	in	sack
bat	jacks	San
can	jam	sax
cap	Jan	ten
cat	mitt	van
fan	not	yak
gas	pack	yam
ham	pan	

Sight Words

a	some
do	the
go	we
I	what
put	you
see	

Challenge Word

ball

Extension Activities

Discussion Questions

- What do you think Dad expects San to pack?
- What do you think San should pack?
- What do you like to pack when you take a trip?

Exploring the Story

- Gather several of the following items: large paper bag, jacks, paper fan, hat or cap, small pan, picture of San's dad, can, rag, lid, mitt, cup, and nut. Place them on the table, saying each item's name. Pack the bag with things that have the short *a* sound.
- Write the following letters on separate sheets of large paper: *a*, *b*, *c*, *g*, *m*, *n*, *p*, *s*, *t*.
- Tape the letters to the floor in a grid, as shown below. Have a child stand on the letter *a*. Call out one of the following words and have the child, using hands or a foot, touch the other two letters found in the word: *bam*, *ban*, *bat*, *cab*, *cam*, *can*, *cap*, *cat*, *gab*, *gap*, *gas*, *man*, *map*, *mat*, *nab*, *nag*, *nap*, *pan*, *pat*, *sag*, *San*, *sat*, *tab*, *tag*, *tam*, *tan*, *tap*.
- Children can play this game in pairs once they are comfortable with the process.

b	p	g
c	a	n
s	m	t